THE LITTLE BOOK

WITH A

BIG VOICE

SECOND EDITION

Christopher Hiedeman

ChristopherHiedeman.com

CONTENTS

.

THE WISHING WELL

Once upon a time, deep in the woods outside of a little town called Zelvish, there was a wishing well. The wishing well was buried in decades of dead branches and brush. It was a magical well that had been forgotten long ago.

The town of Zelvish, though they had all the space they needed, decided to expand. They cut down the trees in the woods and cleared them away, getting the land ready for more businesses. A few days into their demolition, they uncovered the well. At first, the workers were ready to demolish it. But a golden sign on the well caught their attention, so they took a break from their duties to see what it said.

The Wishing Well

This well was made with love, with a heart for giving. Lower the pail into the well, and whatever you wish will materialize in the pail. This well is meant only to be used as necessary and cannot supply money. Overuse will cause it to wither away.

The workers laughed at the well, for how could such a thing exist? As a joke, one worker lowered the pail into the well and wished for a new pair of shoes. When the pail was raised back up, resting neatly in the pail was a new pair of leather shoes. The workers' laughing ceased. One by one they tested the well, and one by one they received the gift they desired.

That evening, the workers told their families about the well, and over the next few days, the entire town of Zelvish knew about the wishing well. A long line formed at the wishing well, as people wished for things they didn't at all need, but wanted nonetheless.

Outside of the town of Zelvish lay a little farm. The family that lived there was poor and would sometimes go days without much to eat. Cindy, the eldest daughter, heard about the wishing well at school one day and decided to check it out after classes.

As afternoon approached, Cindy walked over to the edge of town and got in the mile-long line for the well. Hours and hours went by as she watched people skip by her with brand-new ruby earrings, fancy purses, and other luxuries. Cindy thought hard about what she would wish for. She wanted nothing for herself but something to help her family instead. Maybe some food, she thought. Maybe some vegetable seeds so they could grow a garden. Her little brother needed shoes; maybe that is what she should wish for. She spent the next hour dreaming of what she should wish for to give to her family.

She was the third person in line and patiently waited to meet the magical well. The person in front of her stepped forward, and so did she. Cindy looked at the woman in front of her, who wore a fancy dress and was adorned with exquisite jewelry.

The woman walked up to the well and said, "I want a diamond necklace."

Cindy watched in awe as the woman lifted a sparkling necklace out of the pail. The woman stood aside and began attempting to put the necklace around her neck. Cindy walked up to the wishing well and sifted through her many wishes in her mind. She wanted so badly to give everything she could to her family but didn't know what her wish should be. She finally settled on some food for her family. She thought to herself how excited her parents and little brother would be to have a good meal on the table for supper. She smiled and asked the well, "Could I please have some food for my family?"

As per the instructions on the well's golden sign, Cindy lowered the pail into the well and brought it back up to her. The pail was empty. Sadness filled her heart as disappointment flooded her thoughts. She read the sign once more to see if she did something wrong and read:

> *This well is meant only to be used as necessary and cannot supply money. Overuse will cause it to wither away.*

That was it, she thought. Unfortunately, the well was used faster than it could replenish itself, and now, it had gone dry.

It was almost dark. She was disappointed that she wasn't able to give something nice to her family. But she put a smile on her face and walked home.

Time passed, and the whole town of Zelvish learned that the once-magical well was not magical anymore.

A few weeks passed. Cindy sat outside, enjoying the warm summer day. A cool breeze swept across the plains. A piece of paper drifted through the air in the distance and landed on the ground next to her. The parchment was old and stained. In curiosity, she flipped it over to see what it was.

Dear Giver,

Thank you for visiting the wishing well. By now, I am certain the well has been found and that it has most likely dried up.

The well was not intended for frivolous use but was built to help others—to give to those in need. But, unfortunately, much of this world only knows how to take.

You are receiving this letter because of your extraordinarily selfless, giving heart. You have been chosen to be the new keeper of a wishing well. Follow the instructions below to build your own wishing well.

Use it wisely. Help others who need it. By giving to others, you will enjoy a fortune the selfish takers will never know of.

Thank you.

Kindly,

Wishing Well Keeper CCXXXII

THE LAST EMPATH

Of all the wonders of the world headed for extinction, one of the kindest and most caring beings was nearing its life's end. Over the many centuries of the Empath's existence, the world had changed. He spent the last century searching the world and came to the saddening conclusion that empathy no longer existed in others. The kind and caring world had become cold and selfish. Though his time was limited, the Empath could not bear to leave the world in the state it was in, for inevitably, the world was headed to its end if left this way. So, with a loving heart, he made one last promise to the world he loved—that he would work tirelessly to restore empathy to the world until his last dying breath.

While walking down the street, he came across a young man and felt a coldness around him. The Empath tripped and fell to the ground before the young man as a test, but the young man carried on with little caring. The Empath got up, walked up to the young man, and placed his hand on the young man's shoulder. In an instant, the world's surroundings disappeared leaving just the young man and the Empath. The young man turned around and looked at the Empath.

"Hey!" he said hastily.

"What is your name, son?" asked the Empath.

"Trevor—why do you want to know?" he responded.

"I have—"

"Where am I?" interrupted Trevor as he looked around at the blank surroundings.

"Trevor," the Empath began again, "I have chosen you, because you, like so many others in this world have unkindly judged another human being."

"So what!" responded Trevor angrily. "Who cares."

For a moment, the Empath thought about letting Trevor go back to his unhappy existence, but alas, he cared too much. "I want to show you something," said the Empath, and before Trevor had a chance to decline his offer, the Empath rested his hand on the shoulder of the young man, and they were transported to a sidewalk outside a noisy bar.

"Recognize this place?" asked the Empath.

"Sure. Why does it matter—I haven't been here for a few years," replied Trevor in a snarky voice.

The Empath looked at Trevor with kind eyes and said, "Follow me."

Trevor hesitated for a moment but, seeing the Empath waiting with the door open, decided to humor him.

They walked into the bar, and Trevor froze in his footsteps. He saw a past version of himself drinking at the bar. "Wait a minute…did we…?"

"I have brought you back in the past to take a closer look at this day, for even though this day doesn't seem significant, it may change your life," said the Empath as he pointed at the bar.

They both watched as Past Trevor drank beer after beer. Trevor looked over at the Empath and began fidgeting. "So I had a few drinks," he said defensively. "Don't judge!"

The Empath said nothing but smirked slightly for Trevor had unknowingly uncovered the lesson he was supposed to learn. "Look at the guy next to you—he seems to be having a few drinks too," said the Empath. Trevor looked over at the man with red hair and green glasses. He had a tattoo of a sparrow on his right arm.

"Yeah…" Trevor responded.

After a few more beers, Past Trevor got up from his chair and stumbled toward the door. The Empath gestured for Trevor to follow his past self. Once outside, Past Trevor walked over to a black car and got in. "Let's go!" said the Empath. They rushed to the car and got into the back seat.

"I know what you're going to say," said Trevor, "but I can drive fine when I have had a few drinks."

"Whatever you say," responded the Empath.

The car peeled out as Past Trevor made his way out of the parking lot and down the road to go home. He weaved down the road crossing the centerline when suddenly headlights burst from the other side of the road. Their car swerved back into the lane just in time. Trevor sunk into his seat beside the Empath. He couldn't believe how close he had gotten to hitting that other car.

Trevor looked over at the Empath embarrassed and said, "I get it; it won't happen again."

The Empath looked kindly at Trevor. "That is good, but this is not the lesson I have brought you here to learn."

Trevor looked at the Empath in confusion, then looked forward.

When the car stopped, the Empath and Trevor exited the vehicle and went into the house. The Empath rested on the couch as Past Trevor went upstairs. "So what do we do now?" he asked.

"We go to sleep," said the Empath.

Trevor wanted to ask a follow-up question but instead decided to lie down.

Bright sunlight burst through the living room windows as the sun rose into the sky. Past Trevor came bustling down the stairs quickly. Trevor looked up at his past self with confusion. "Wait…what year is this?" he asked.

"Actually, we are only ten days from the present," the Empath responded.

They were in a different year than when they went to bed the night before. "It's time," said the Empath as he watched Past Trevor walking out of the house.

They got into the back seat of the car once more and observed Past Trevor as he drove to work. The car came to a stop at a red traffic light. A homeless man wandered up to the front driver's-side window. Past Trevor rolled his window down.

"Can I get a little money for some food?" asked the homeless man with hopeful eyes.

"Get a job!" yelled Past Trevor before rolling his window back up. The traffic light turned green. Trevor leaned over to the window to get a closer look at the man and his heart sank. There sitting on the curb was a man with red hair wearing a broken pair of green glasses. Trevor stared out the back window as they drove away.

"That's the guy from the bar, isn't it?" asked Trevor.

"Yes, it is," replied the Empath calmly. "And wouldn't you know—that same night, he too drove home drunk, but instead, he did crash his car on his way home."

Trevor looked at the Empath with haunted eyes.

"His car was totaled, and his medical bills piled up after his accident. He eventually lost his home, and because of this, he also lost his job."

After he spoke of this revelation, the Empath heard the silence in the air but felt its necessity.

"I…I had no idea," said Trevor humbly.

The Empath looked at Trevor and thoughtfully said, "Isn't it interesting that, really, that could have been you?"

Trevor took a moment to reflect on this. He was truly lucky he didn't get into a car accident that night. The Empath was right—that could have been him. Something changed in his heart as he opened himself up to the possibilities of what that man had been through, and what that man was still going through.

A tear sailed down Trevor's cheek, and just like that, the Empath saw the small spark of empathy in Trevor's heart grow into a beaming sun of warmth and caring.

"Thank you so much," said Trevor with a warm smile. "I will never forget this."

The Empath smiled at him, and they embraced in a hug.

Trevor felt the presence of the Empath vanish. He opened his eyes, and there he was, back in the present. He paused for a moment, trying to remember what he was doing. He remembered that he was on his way to buy an expensive pair of shoes he had been eyeballing for a while. He looked up into the sky and smiled.

Trevor burst out running in the other direction. He felt the wind whispering past his ears as he sprinted through town. He turned a corner, and there across the street from him was the homeless man. When the traffic light turned red, Trevor crossed the street and walked up to him. The man looked at Trevor with uncertainty.

"I wanted to apologize for my behavior before…I don't know if you remember me…if you don't, it is probably for the best," said Trevor with a nervous smile.

Trevor held out his hand and shook the homeless man's rough hand. Trevor could see the man had learned his lesson and was now just trying to get his life back on track. Trevor reached into his pocket and lifted out the $200 cash that he was going to use to buy himself a pair of shoes he didn't need. He handed the cash to the homeless man and said, "Here you go."

A large smile spread across the homeless man's face. Tears welled up in his eyes. "Are you sure?" he asked.

"Positive," replied Trevor with a warm smile. He shook the man's hand once more, then began to walk home. He originally was going to buy expensive shoes so he would feel good about himself, but the feeling he got by giving was more powerful than anything he had ever experienced. The rest of the day, Trevor could not stop smiling. He felt better about himself than he had ever felt before. He was happy to help another person. The Empath had taught him a valuable lesson that he would not soon forget: We cannot know what another person is going through or what had led them to where they are in life. We can only hope for better days for them.

It is not always about the decisions we make but sometimes the luck we have that keeps us from unfortunate effects of our actions.

A small spark of empathy was set out into the world to ignite caring and kindness once more. Though it was near extinction, it just took the heart of one soul to keep the torch ablaze to be passed on and light up the world again.

20 MORE YEARS

A young woman looked into a mirror. She was in her early twenties and judged her appearance daily. Her hair was too curly. She wasn't as skinny as she wanted to be. She looked upon herself with harsh eyes as she fussed over her hair and makeup in an attempt to make herself more beautiful. One night, after another session of critical judgment, she went to bed and fell fast asleep.

The next morning, she woke up and began her day as usual. She went into the kitchen to grab the low-fat cereal out of the cupboard. As she raised her arm for the cupboard, she glanced at her skin, which had sagged slightly. In a panic, she ran to the bathroom and looked in the mirror. She looked as if she had aged twenty years overnight. She looked around her and noticed that she had not been the only one aging—her home had aged as well. The woman ran into the kitchen in a panic and looked at the calendar to reveal twenty years had passed.

She stood there stunned, trying to make sense of this. How could twenty years have passed by so fast? She paced the room for about an hour before she slowly walked back into the bathroom. She switched on the light and hesitantly raised her head to look at herself once more. In the mirror was a woman in her forties. Her face had fine lines, and her hair wasn't as buoyant as it used to be. She looked at this image with dissatisfaction, then went about her day.

She went to work like she always had. The only thing that seemed to have changed was the age of her coworkers. It took her a good month to get used to her new life.

While rummaging through her house, she found an old photo of herself from her twenties and thought to herself, Wow. I was actually kind of pretty. She stared at the photograph, reminiscing of those days. She set the photograph down and went on with her day.

She had just finished cleaning the house, and suddenly the phone rang; it was her parents. She chatted with her mom for a while and then made up a quick excuse to get off the phone. She loved her mom, but surely, they could chat some other time. She just wanted to relax in peace and watch TV. So that is what she did.

A few days later, her parents called her again, and again she made up an excuse to limit the length of the phone call. She had so many things she wanted to do—and chatting on the phone for hours wasn't one of them. After she finished her shows, she cleaned up and went to bed.

The next morning, she woke up and went to use the bathroom. She turned on the light and jumped. She looked into the mirror, and a woman in her sixties looked back at her. No! she thought. This can't be!

Again, she ran into the kitchen to look at her calendar, and again, twenty years had gone by. She walked back into the bathroom and looked at herself in the mirror once more. She saw more wrinkles on herself. How is this happening? she wondered.

After coming to terms with her new change, she went to work. When she arrived, she looked around and recognized very few people. "Oh, hi!" said a voice from behind her. "We haven't seen you since your retirement party—I think it has been a good five years!"

Retired? she thought. She smiled at the person and left suddenly to go home. Time really has flown by, she thought. When she got home, she sat down to watch TV—and that is what she did with her days.

She looked outside at the beautiful days but instead spent her time watching TV indoors.

She grew lonely and wondered if her parents would call. She brought her phone by her and sat next to it— just in case they called her. A month went by with no calls. She decided to give her parents a call. She dialed the number and listened to the phone ring. A young man picked up the phone and said "Hello?"

"Hi," she said, not recognizing the voice.

"This is James; can I help you with something?"

"I think I have the wrong number; I was trying to reach my parents," she said.

The young man went on to describe how he and his wife had purchased the house twelve years ago, after an estate sale. She slammed down the phone in a panic. She tried calling her aunt, and again, she had the wrong number.

She raced into the kitchen to find her book of phone numbers and saw a dusty, warped card sitting atop her fridge. She lifted it down to look at it. It was a sympathy card. She opened the card, and tears welled up in her eyes as she read it. Her parents had passed away. She sat on the floor and sobbed, wishing she had spent more time with them when she had had a chance.

The days went by, and she continued her routine of TV watching. The weather was beautiful, but she didn't feel like going outside. I can do that any day, she thought.

That night she went to bed and fell asleep.

Bright sunlight beamed through the window and woke her. She started to get out of bed but had a little trouble getting up. She set her hand on her side table and used it to help her stand up. Once upright, she walked into the bathroom. She turned on the light to reveal an eighty-year-old woman staring back at her. She stood there slightly out of breath and, with little care for this new change, walked into the living room.

She sat down on the sofa and maneuvered herself so that the springs were not poking her. She turned on the TV and watched a show. She was tired of many things and was tired of watching TV. I should go for a walk, she thought to herself.

The sun was bright and cheery outside; it was a truly beautiful day. She started to get up but had trouble. She reached to each side of her to find something to help her up. She finally scooted over to the side of the sofa next to the side table and used it to help her get up.

The woman stood there slightly out of breath. She began walking toward the door, but her knees hurt. She made it to the door and out onto the first step. It was a glorious day, but, sadly, she was too sore and tired to enjoy it.

She thought to herself about all the sunny days she stayed inside watching TV shows. Her heart sank as she walked back into the house and closed the door. She was afraid to sit on the couch again for she had so much trouble getting up last time. She stood in the middle of the living room and cried.

Why didn't I go outside and enjoy it while I still could?

Why hadn't I spent more time with my family while they were still here?

Why did I judge myself so harshly when in all truth, I was beautiful?

She walked back into her bedroom and lay down. Tears crept down her face as she thought about her past and how she wished she could do it all over again. She slowly cried herself into a deep sleep.

The next morning, she woke up. Half asleep, she wandered into the bathroom and turned on the light. She looked into the mirror, and there, standing in front of her, was a beautiful young woman with her whole life ahead of her. She had a new appreciation for her health, a new love for her family, and a new love for herself.

FAKE: THE MAKING OF PERFECTION

After another successfully polished image of her "perfect" table setting was posted, Valerie set down her phone and let her family sit down to a now-cold, mostly home-cooked meal.

"How was school today?" she asked, smiling at her youngest son, Trevor, who picked at his meal.

Trevor looked up at her with unhappy eyes and said nothing. He was angry with his mom, who was supposed to pick him up from school earlier that day. She instead made him ride the bus, because she was too busy taking photos of her new living-room furniture to post online.

"How about you, honey? How was your day?" asked Valerie, looking at her husband, Josh.

He shook his head and replied, "It was just…just fine." Josh stood up hastily, walked into the kitchen, and put his plate in the microwave. He slammed the microwave door shut, trying to make a statement to his wife, but unfortunately the gesture was lost on her. She was too busy trying to take a quick photo of the sunset through the window.

The two of them didn't speak much to each other anymore. Valerie's life online didn't interest her husband, but that was all she wanted to talk about anymore.

Valerie scrolled through the photos she had posted, smiling at all the compliments she got from her followers. She felt like a celebrity and craved more of that feeling. From airbrushed photos of her "flawless" makeup to forced family moments, each photo gave her followers a small glimpse into her "perfect" life.

Her life online, though, was nothing but fake. She was so used to living these lies that she had started to believe her life was perfect.

One evening, her husband came home from work as she stood in the kitchen taking another selfie to share with her followers. Josh set his briefcase on the counter and walked up to her.

"Can we talk?" he asked with sadness in his eyes.

Valerie didn't break eye contact with her phone and said, "Just a minute."

Josh waited for a few minutes. "Seriously, Val, can we talk?"

Valerie broke her stare from her phone and said, "Oh my God, *what!*"

He looked at her with hurt eyes that began to well up with tears.

"Val…I want a divorce."

Valery smirked. "What? What do you mean you want a div—"

"We haven't been happy for a long time."

"I have been happy," said Valerie.

"OK, well *I* haven't."

The room was silent for a moment. "All you ever do anymore is spend time on your phone, and I'm sick of it. You care more about your followers than you do your own family. I am tired of being second place in your life." Tears poured down Josh's face.

Valerie looked at him shocked. "But—"

"Do you realize those photos you share aren't even real? Where are the photos of you holding Trevor when he was born? You hide all the parts of your life that make it *living*."

"I wasn't even wearing makeup that day," she said angrily.

"You were the most beautiful woman in the world that day."

Stunned, she stood there, lost for words for a moment.

"I...I just want people t...to like me," said Valerie as she looked at her husband through glazed eyes.

"But we, your family, like you. In fact, we love you. Isn't that enough?"

Josh left the room, leaving her in an uncomfortable silence. Valerie picked up her phone from the counter and with shaking hands, scrolled through the photos. She felt as if she was seeing them through fresh eyes, and her husband was right. None of it was real. The photos were so polished and staged that, really, they were fake.

She held her phone up in front of her, clicked the camera icon, and looked at herself. Mascara lines ran down her face, and her eyes were puffy. She snapped a photo, and before she posted it, she wrote:

Dear followers,

Thank you for always having my back. I feel like I haven't been honest with you. I don't always have perfect hair, and most days at home, I don't even wear makeup. My home isn't always clean and tidy, and sometimes my cooking doesn't turn out. If it is OK with you, I would like to start sharing my real life with you—unedited, no-filter.

I have made a real mess of my life chasing after perfection. Some parts of life are not polished, but that doesn't make those moments any less beautiful.

Signing off for a while to spend time with my family.

Love always,

Valerie

THE RICHEST

Two couples lived next door to each other. The house on the left towered over its neighbor to the right. It was a large house with wondrous landscaping, fountains, and an outdoor pool. The house on the right was just a small bungalow with a plain front lawn.

Though the couple on the left had many luxuries, they were never home to enjoy them. The wife had a successful job in advertising, and her husband was a doctor. Both spent most of their days at their jobs and little time at home with family or each other.

The couple in the house on the right spent a lot of their time at home. They worked at their day jobs and then spent the rest of their days home together playing games, watching movies, and conversing. They did not have money for the luxuries their neighbors had, but they were happy, so it didn't bother them.

As the years went by, the couple in the house on the left grew more and more wealthy. But they spent less and less time with each other and their family.

Their neighbors' finances were unchanged, as were their house and lawn.

Though they were neighbors, they only saw small glimpses of each other's lives and would smile and wave at each other on occasion. The couple on the right was in awe of the couple on the left's life. They watched new luxury cars come and go, as well as larger and larger TVs. Though they admired these luxuries, they were happy with their life that they shared together as a couple and with their family.

The couple on the left envied the couple on the right. When they were off to work or meetings, they would catch glimpses of romantic dinners or family celebrations. They would look fondly at their neighbors' house during the holidays—full of decorations and family. Though contrary to the public eye, the couple on the left did not think of themselves as successful. No matter how much money they had, no matter how many luxuries they accumulated, deep down, they felt poor somehow. The world had taught them that money equaled success and that success equaled happiness. But as the years passed, the couple on the left found this to be untrue. Though their neighbors to the right had very little, their life was full of riches that money couldn't buy. Their neighbors' lives were full of moments and memories.

So the couple on the left decided it was time to retire. They left their jobs and put their large house up for sale. After the sale of their house, they started the process of moving. The couple had purchased a home closer to their family where they could spend their remaining years.

The last moving truck was ready to leave, and so were they. Before they left, they walked over to their neighbors' house and knocked on the door. The door opened to reveal a woman and man, who smiled and said, "Hello!"

"Hi," said the wife on the doorstep. "We just wanted to say thank you."

The wife in the house looked at the woman on the step. "For what?" she said with curiosity.

"Though we really have never talked with either of you much, we have admired your lives. You both are always smiling and seem very happy. I would look over at your house during the holidays and see a house full of people. With our jobs, we really didn't have much time for our family. In fact, we spent most of our holidays alone—sometimes at our jobs." Her eyes started to tear up slightly as she continued, "All these years I had the wrong definition of success in my head. Thank you both for this priceless gift."

They embraced in a warm hug, smiled, and waved at each other one last time. The couple moved into their new small house—one that finally felt like a home. They spent most of their time with family and friends and more time with each other.

The richest of us are not those with the most money but those with the most memories.

SHE KNOWS

I looked over at my beloved wife. Time had been kind to us both, but sadly, it was running out. Even though Edith and I were in our nineties, we felt as young as we ever had inside. When I look at her, I see a beautiful woman. The same woman I fell in love with years and years ago. It is funny—though our bodies age, our minds stay young. When you get to be as old as I am, your perspective on attractiveness changes. You no longer judge others' looks. You grow to learn that it is the heart that is important, nothing more.

Edith and I have lived a very full and wondrous life together. Like any couple, we had our differences in opinions, but we talked and worked through them. On occasion, young couples would ask us, "What is your secret? What has kept your relationship going all of these years?"

I would answer, "Isn't it obvious? Love. Unconditional love."

You see, so many people in the world today don't know what unconditional love is. For most people, love always has conditions. You will only give love if your partner stays thin. You will only give love as long as your finances are comfortable. People place so many silent conditions on their love for the other person that inevitably, their relationships come to an end before "till death do us part."

As I look into the fading eyes of my wife, I feel a great love for her. The same unconditional love we have shared all these years. You would think, knowing I only had minutes left with her that there would be so much left to say. But that is the thing— I already said it. She knows how beautiful she is. She knows how smart she is. She knows how kind and caring she is. She knows how much I appreciate her, and she knows I love her deeply. And because she knows this, I know she knows that I will never forget her. At death, we may part hands, but we will never part hearts.

A WONDROUS LIFE

Sarah sat next to the window. It was cloudy outside, and somehow the gloominess crept into her head, clouding her thoughts and darkening her inner peace. It was just one of those days.

So much seemed so wrong in her life. She watched the rain race down the windowpane like tears as she thought about all of the negative things in her life. She couldn't help it. It seemed that each time she pulled her focus to something positive, the world found a way to push her off her feet and send her crashing to the ground once more. She was getting tired of fighting with these thoughts and began thinking of a way out. She thought about how this "way out" would teach her unreasonable boss a lesson. How it would be one final slap in the face to her ex-husband. So Sarah took a bottle of pills and got comfortable on her bed, ready to say good-bye to all of her problems. With shaking hands, she lifted a handful of pills up, but before she could take them, a woman walked into the room.

She quickly stashed the pills under her pillow and said, "Who are you? What are you doing here?"

The woman walked up to her side and said, "I know what you are about to do. Honestly, I am not here to stop you, but I am here to make sure you understand fully what you are about to do."

"I won't change my mind," Sarah said firmly.

The woman smiled at her and held out her hand. "Will you follow me please?"

Sarah hesitated for a second, then got up and walked up to the woman. She followed the woman as she walked through the house. They entered a room with four doors within it. "Where did this room come from?" she asked, looking around the room confused.

The woman pointed at the door on the left and said, "Let's start with this one."

Hesitantly, she walked over to it and opened it. Her mother stood in a kitchen next to her childhood self, baking cookies. "Momma loves you!" her mother said, giving Sarah's younger self a kiss, followed by a big hug. Sarah stood in the doorway and watched a smile spread across her childhood self's face, followed by a joyous laugh. They continued rolling the chocolate-chip cookie dough into little balls and placing them onto the baking sheet. Sarah smiled and watched. She loved her mother. She had forgotten about this day. The memories of that fun day came flooding back to her.

The woman tapped on her shoulder and said, "It's time to see what is behind the next door."

"OK," said Sarah. She walked over to the next door and opened it to see sleeping bags spread out across the living-room floor of their old house. Sarah watched as a younger version of herself came bouncing into the room, followed by three of her best friends.

They spent the evening playing board games and talking about everything imaginable. One of her friends, Carlie, put her hand out and said, "OK, you guys, pinky promise we will always be friends!"

The girls ran over to her giggling as they put their hands together. "I love you guys!" said Sarah's past self to the smiling girls around her.

Sarah watched these moments like a movie she never wanted to end. But again, the woman gestured for her to open the next door.

Behind the third door was a sunny day at the beach with her grandpa. "Grandpa! Grandpa! Watch this!" her younger self said with excitement. Her grandpa looked in her direction as she attempted to stand up on her inner tube. She slipped and fell through the center of her inner tube. She coughed as she went underwater. Sarah watched as her grandpa came running to help her out of her inner tube.

"Are you OK, my dear?" he asked with concern.

After she stopped coughing, she nodded. Her grandpa gave her a big hug. "Thank you, Papa!" she said.

They walked back onto the sandy beach, and he wrapped her in a cozy oversized towel.

Sarah felt the woman tap on her shoulder once more. It was time to open the final door. Expecting another moment with family or friends, Sarah opened the fourth door to reveal a mirror. She looked through the door at herself standing there with her hand on the doorknob. "I…I don't get it," she said.

Sarah saw the woman walk up beside her. "Now that you have opened all of these doors, it is time for you to make your choice. If you are truly ready to leave all of this behind, close the doors."

Sarah looked at herself in the mirror and grasped the doorknob tightly. She couldn't break eye contact with herself. Her eyes glazed over as she looked at the woman that stood before her. "I…I can't do it," she said. Tears rolled off her face and speckled her shirt.

"Why is that?" asked the woman

Sarah thought about this question, and it moved her. She looked into the mirror and said, "Because until now, I hadn't taken the time to actually think about it, but I realize now—I love myself too much."

The room was silent. She sat on the floor in front of the mirror and cried. She sat there and thought about all the happy moments that the woman had shown her. She wasn't ready to close the door on any of it. She loved her family, she loved her friends, and she loved herself.

Sarah stood up and collected herself.

"Thank…you," she said, looking around the room for the woman, but the woman was gone. She turned and looked into the mirror once more and smiled. Though sometimes her life seemed dark, the darkness was nothing compared to the light that was cast upon her by her family and friends. She did indeed have a wondrous life, and she wasn't ready to give that up.

GRAY

Aster looked out the window. Colorful houses lined busy streets full of people. Each person cast their personal style on the world around them, creating a sea of interesting, vibrant beauty.

She sat back in her rocking chair. Her grandchildren came running up to her.

"Grandma! Grandma!"

A smile formed on Aster's face. "What is it, my darlings?"

"Tell us a story," they asked eagerly.

Aster pondered for a moment, then looked at her grandchildren and smiled. "You know, I have just the story for you," she said. She glanced out the window once more and began.

Once upon a time, the world was not like it is today. Houses used to be painted mostly the same colors, and people used to dress in mostly the same clothes. They read mostly the same books and watched mostly the same movies. Having your own personal style back then was frowned upon. Society had come to the conclusion that similarity was preferred over difference, and so, the world was bland.

One day, a young girl was born. Her parents decided to raise her to be strong; they raised her to be herself. So she was. Being herself was not always easy—actually, most of the time, it was quite difficult. She dressed in bright colors unlike the other girls and boys at school. She loved to create things, while others around her frowned upon her creativity. Though the world seemed against her dreams, her parents encouraged her to follow her heart—and so she did.

After she graduated from school, she had a hard time getting on her feet. Though she knew her work was valuable to the world, the world was stubborn to see the value in her work.

Her parents reassured her, telling her—

> *Just because it hasn't been done before doesn't mean it shouldn't be done. The world cannot be changed with old ideas and old ways.*

Now a young woman, she took life by the reins and followed her heart. She dreamed of a world full of color—a world that celebrated difference—and so she made it her mission to change the world.

She began writing about uniqueness and paid to have her writing printed in the local newspaper. She did this for a few weeks, until one day the newspaper contacted her and asked if she would write a segment in the paper weekly. They told her they had had such an overwhelming warm response from readers that they would like to pay her to write rather than have her paying to write.

She jumped at the opportunity with excitement and continued writing about uniqueness in her segment titled "How To Be Yourself." She received warm responses from people of all ages and found that, though sometimes she felt alone by being herself, many people yearned to be themselves but were too scared to stray from the gray world.

Over the years, something marvelous started happening. The world started to change. People started painting their houses different colors. They started wearing unique clothing, reading different books, and watching movies that interested them. The world wasn't just becoming a different place but a happier place. People were being themselves—they were happier because they were no longer trying so hard to be something that they were not.

By straying from the gray ways of the world, she brightened the lives of those around her.

Aster looked down at her grandchildren's faces and saw their eyes filled with wonder. She smiled, for she was happy with the vibrant world that they would experience.

She glanced over at a framed article she had on the wall beside her and read the final line of the article:

> *Be a bright beacon of color and wash the world in beauty; life's too short to live life without **color**.*

THE SILENCE.

When I was younger, I never appreciated the noise. All the noise annoyed me, so I tried my best to get away from it as often as I could. Life had such a deafening sound – people talking to me constantly, needing me for this, that, and the other things. I grew tired of it and just wanted to run away from it all. I was sick of the scheduled get-togethers. I was sick of the obligations. Today though, I don't feel that way anymore. I miss the noise.

As you grow with time, you learn life's saddest lesson: the noise is not infinite. As time goes on, the noise dissipates. People move away and lose touch, and hardest of all, people pass away. Those annoying phone calls become fewer and fewer, until one day, you find yourself in a lonely silence.

Though the noise in my life is less today, I have gone out in search of new music for this new part of my life. As with the noise, silence can be deafening too – even more so. Daily silence isn't the key to a happy life; I know that now. I started getting out more often and meeting new people, and wouldn't you know, my life wasn't as silent anymore. I began reaching out to those in my life who had moved away, and surprisingly, they began to call more often.

This new life sound is a different one than the sound I remember, but it is music to my ears. It can never replace the noise I remember in my youth; nostalgia is a powerful thing. But, it is never too late to make new friendships and to reconnect with those in our past we can still reach.

So, my lesson for you is this: embrace the noise! It is one of life's gifts that many don't appreciate. Though life can seem loud at times, just remember, it is a joyous melody that cannot last exactly the same forever. So enjoy the noise life blesses you with each day - there will never be a noise just like it.

TEN YEARS AGO

Ten years ago, I met the love of my life.

I met a reflection of myself - a reflection of every piece of me that was who I was. By reflection, I don't mean we were exactly alike. We were alike in all the ways that mattered the most. We both loved our family, and we both were compassionate and giving. We both saw the value in keeping a neat home, and we both saw the value in taking care of what we had. We were a reflection of each other's underlying values. Beyond that, we were quite different from each other – we each had talents in different areas of life and living. We had our own types and libraries of knowledge. What I have learned over the past years, is that we not only found each other to love, but we each found our missing part. We were great on our own, but as a team, we are our greatest; we bring out the best in each other.

Pretending that we never had disagreements would be a lie. I believe our love has lasted because we love each other enough to talk to each other until we understand each other. Over the last ten years, we have never stopped talking. When we disagree on something, we talk until we reach an understanding – no matter how late it is, or how long it takes. We are each human beings with different pasts, giving us different ways of looking at the world. These differences can be a good thing – they can teach the other person a perspective they may not have considered before. Disagreements don't have to be fights; they can be productive discussions that bring you closer together as a couple. The more discussions you have with each other through life, the more your paths move toward each other. When you have these discussions, you are talking with your partner- your teammate. Love is not about competition. It isn't about winning. It is about understanding and growing closer to each other.

Ten years later, I can't help but smile whenever we are together. Each time we hold hands, I have an inner scream of joy. Each time we hug, I never want to let go. I close my eyes and feel an indescribable happiness. I feel I'm exactly where I need to be.

Ten years ago, I fell in love with a kind soul. I fell in love with a beautiful mind and a caring heart. Over the years, though I didn't think it was possible, our love continues to grow even deeper.

Love has nothing to do with finances. Love has nothing to do with looks. Love is about the soul – it is about personality.

I am grateful more than words can express for our love. It was a pleasant surprise, an unexpected gift that I will always cherish.

SOMETHING BETTER

The phone rang incessantly on the nightstand. Sarah checked her phone – it was Gwen, her mother. She decided not to answer the call and just let it go to voicemail.

Her mother tried calling and texting her a few times a month, but Sarah found this annoying. Her mother always wanted to schedule time to see her, but Sarah had so many things she would rather do with her time. When her mother would ask her about a certain date, she would simply reply, "I don't know if I can. I will let you know when I know for sure."

Sarah's mother grew to expect this response, but never-the-less, she was silently excited inside for the possibility of them spending time together. She fantasized about the fun new memories they would make together, and even though she only received a "maybe," she began planning their time together.

The date was getting close. Sarah didn't want to cement her plans with her mother because there was a chance she might get to go out with her friend Lexie that day. She didn't want to say no to her mom though – she didn't want to spend that Saturday by herself either.

It was Friday night. Gwen sat by her phone on pins and needles, hoping for a phone call from her daughter saying they would be spending Saturday together. The phone rang, and Gwen answered quickly. It was Gwen's close friend Megan. Megan asked if she had any plans the next day. Megan was looking for someone to go shopping with her. Gwen explained to her friend that she might have plans with her daughter, so she would have to pass. They said their goodbyes and hung up. Gwen continued to sit by the phone, waiting for her daughter to call and give her news either way.

Morning sunlight shined on her face and woke her. Gwen had fallen asleep on the sofa with the phone next to her. She picked it up quickly to see if she had any missed calls but there were none. Gwen picked up the phone and called her daughter. She got Sarah's voicemail. With hesitation, she decided to leave a message.

Beep

"Hi Sarah honey. It's Mom. I was hoping to hear from you last night. I didn't know if you were planning on spending time with me today or not.

You know, sweetie, it's ok if you don't want to spend time with me, just tell me. I know that going through old photos, and having lunch and coffee together is probably not on the top of the list of things you wanted to do with your Saturday – but someday, you will know why times like this are so special. There will come a day when..."

Gwen started to tear up a little.

"There will come a day when I am no longer here. There will come a day when I won't be able to just call you – a day when you won't just be a phone call away from me... You have much more time left on this earth than I do, and if you have time, I would like to spend as much of my time left with you as I can."

Gwen trembled with the phone in her hand. "Love you, sweetie! OK, bye-bye."

While her mother poured her heart out into the voicemail, for the fourth time that week, Sarah spent the day with her friend Lexie – shopping for more clothes she didn't need. Sarah heard the voicemail ping sound on her phone. She checked it to see if it was another one of her friends, but when she saw it was her mom, she ignored it. She could listen to that some other time. Sarah and Lexie went about their day of shopping.

Gwen set the phone down, happy that she had finally told her daughter how these actions made her feel. She hoped it would be a turning point in their distant relationship, but unfortunately, like many of her daughter's messages, it was lost in the sea of incoming notifications she ignored.

Easter was just around the corner, and Gwen wanted to have all the family at her house. She sent out her invitations and heard back from most everyone, except for her daughter. She found this somewhat disappointing, but loved her with all her heart. She let her heart get excited for the time she hoped to spend with her daughter anyway.

Gwen went out and purchased special linens for the table and ordered flowers to make the occasion even more festive. Because of the large crowd she would have, Gwen had to buy extra chairs for the table and quite a bit of extra food. Everything ordered, and the holiday was just around the corner. Gwen looked at her progress, happy with how things were coming together. She was mostly happy to do something fun for her family. Family was the most important thing in life to her.

Saturday night caught up to her fast. She hadn't heard whether her daughter could make it for sure. She decided to give her daughter a call. To Gwen's surprise, Sarah answered.

"Hello?"

"Hi Sarah sweetie!" Gwen exclaimed with delight.

"Oh, hi Mom."

"So honey, can you make it for Easter? I would love it if you could join all of us. Uncle Kevin is going to be here, as well as a few of your cousins."

The phone was silent for a second. "Sure Mom, that sounds like fun."

Fireworks burst inside Gwen's soul. "OK, sweetie! I can't wait!"

"Cool. See you tomorrow then."

"OK, hun. Love you!"

"Yep you too," Sarah replied.

Gwen set the phone down and looked at her home. The decorations made her home festive, but what made the holiday special was the family she would get to spend time with.

The alarm clock went off early Sunday morning. Gwen usually found this sound annoying, but today, it was music to her ears! She was so excited to see her daughter and the rest of her family that she had a hard time sleeping. She got dressed in the special clothes she had set out and put extra care into her hair and makeup.

She started the oven and began preparing the food. She ran between the food and the table, trying to get everything set up and ready. She wanted the day to be absolutely perfect. After a few hours, the doorbell rang. Gwen bounced to the door and opened it with excitement. It was her brother and his two daughters.

"Come on in you guys! Happy Easter!" she said with a large smile on her face.

"Something smells good!"

"Thanks!" she replied. "The ham is cooking in the oven and the potatoes are on their way!"

Her sister walked in. "Oh, your table is absolutely gorgeous!"

Gwen blushed. "Thanks!" she replied with a smile.

"Is Sarah here yet? The girls can't wait to spend time with her."

"Not yet," Gwen replied. She gestured for them to take their seats in the dining room and help themselves to the Easter candy that sat in little decorative dishes next to each plate. "Food shouldn't be too much longer," she said.

Gwen walked into the kitchen and checked her phone, hoping to see a message from her daughter announcing her departure. There were no notifications on her screen though. Gwen looked at the ham and potatoes that were pretty much done cooking. She decided to give her daughter a call. The phone rang a few times and then went to voicemail. Maybe she's driving, Gwen thought. She went back over to the stove to stir the potatoes when she heard her phone make a ting sound. She walked eagerly over to her phone and opened the message.

"Hey Mom. Can't make it. Had to work."

The fireworks that burst in her heart were transformed to rain. She got choked up. She walked into the dining room and said, "Dinner is ready," with a forced smile.

"Shouldn't we wait for Sarah?" her sister asked.

"Sarah just sent me a message saying she can't make it," Gwen responded with sadness.

Her sister paused for a moment, then said, "I was surprised you had said she would be here – Sarah told me there was a concert she wanted to go to today. I thought she might have gotten the days mixed up when you told me she would be here."

Though her daughter's absence upset her, the lie she had told hurt her the most. Why did she promise to visit if she knew she wouldn't make it?

They all sat down to eat. Gwen stared at the empty placemat next to her where her daughter was supposed to be sitting. She burst into tears as she thought about how much her daughter must hate her. Her sister got up and comforted her. "She's just a kid," she said. But Sarah wasn't a kid; she was in her late-twenties. Gwen's tears dried, and she pushed the sadness out of her mind so she could enjoy the rest of her time with the family who wanted to be with her.

The weekend was full of so many laughs and wonderful moments. Her nieces took tons of photos, creating a tangible memory of the beautiful times they all shared together.

A year passed and it was time for Gwen to host her annual Easter dinner again. She went through the list of family she invited each year and paused by her daughter's name. She loved her daughter, but didn't want to invite her, knowing Sarah didn't like spending time with her. So, she skipped inviting Sarah this time. If Sarah called, asking if she could join them, Gwen would gladly accommodate her. But Gwen was tired of inviting Sarah just to have her make up an excuse not to visit.

That Easter came and went. It was less stressful for Gwen, not having to worry about how many guests she would have. Everyone who accepted the invitation to her Easter dinner came to it.

Gwen's phone rang, and she answered. It was Sarah.

"Hi Honey! How are you!"

"I'm good, Mom. Um, I am going to be driving by your place later today and was wondering if I could stay overnight?"

"Sure, sweetie! I can't wait to see you!"

"Yeah. Ok, see you later."

"Ok, hun. Bye," said Gwen with a smile.

"Bye."

Gwen hung up the phone. The feelings inside her were bittersweet. She knew the only reason her daughter was visiting was to save money on the cost of a hotel, and if she wasn't heading through town, she wouldn't be seeing Sarah. Gwen pushed these thoughts out of her head and got excited for her daughter's arrival.

The afternoon turned into evening, and Gwen heard the doorbell ring. She opened the door and it was her daughter Sarah!

"Sweetie! I have missed you so much!" she said.

They embraced in a warm hug, then Sarah continued on inside. She stopped in front of the photo album that rested on the buffet.

"When was this?" Sarah asked.

"Easter," replied Gwen.

Sarah stood quiet for a moment. "Why wasn't I invited?"

Gwen took in a deep breath. "Honey, you know you are always welcome. I have invited you for many holidays and weekends. You always are busy or have some excuse of why you can't make it."

Sarah got ready to interrupt, but Gwen gestured for her to let her finish speaking first.

"I know spending time with your mom is not cool or fun, so I decided, if you didn't want to spend time with me, I would stop making it awkward for you by not inviting you anymore. I don't want to make you come up with excuses all the time – I decided if you really want to see me, you will call me."

Sarah looked at her mother, unsure what to say. She thought about arguing that her excuses were valid. She thought about telling her mom that she takes holidays too seriously.

Gwen looked at Sarah, and with sad eyes said, "If one of your friends said they would go shopping with you, and every time the day came, they wouldn't show or would make up an excuse of why they couldn't make it, how would it make you feel?"

"Well, they probably wouldn't be my friend anymore, and I would never make plans with them again."

After these words left her lips, Sarah thought about them. She began to understand how her mother felt by putting herself in the same situation. She saw the frustration.

"Mom, I'm sorry," she said.

Gwen's eyes welled up with tears. She walked up to her daughter and gave her a big hug. Sarah smiled, for this was the closest she had felt to her Mom in years.

They stayed up and chatted. Sarah and Gwen laughed harder and smiled wider than they had in a long time.

Morning came and Sarah and Gwen said their farewells. Gwen was unsure if anything would permanently change between them, but she was hopeful they would be closer now.

Easter was just around the corner again, and Sarah promised she would be there. Gwen was hesitantly excited for her visit, unsure if it would happen. She and her daughter had conversed more than they ever had throughout the year, but this was the true test.

It was Easter morning. Like usual, Gwen got up early to start cooking and setting the table. Before she got the ham out of the fridge, the doorbell rang. Gwen jumped, almost dropping the ham onto the kitchen floor. She rushed to the door and opened it.

"Happy Easter, Mom!"

Gwen's eyes welled up with tears. Sarah could not know how much this gesture meant to her mother, and really, the gesture was simple.

She wrapped her arms around her daughter with joy and said, "Happy Easter, sweetheart!"

THE GREAT GATHERING

I couldn't believe it! For years and years, I had waited for all my family and friends to get together. This was definitely going to be a joyous reunion!

My grandchildren – oh my grandchildren, how I have missed them! Donna was about fourteen the last time I saw her, and Carson was almost seventeen. When they get passed their teens, they come around less often. I guess spending time with Grandma isn't "hip," but I do miss them and think about them every day.

Anytime now, people should start arriving! I wonder if everyone will make it! I saw my son and daughter-in-law walk by with big platters of sandwiches, and my sister had her famous crockpot chili.

I am so happy that I will get to see all their faces again. I love my family; always have, and always will. I know they love me too, but I wish we had spent more time together through the years. Life has a way of keeping them all busy with their jobs, their own families, and their own gatherings. Sometimes, time can sprint away from us faster than we can chase it.

But that is what is so wonderful about this great big gathering! Not only do I get to see all my loved ones again, but they get to see each other. You see, I think over time, they forget how much they miss each other, and though it is a big job, it is important to get everyone together again to show them what they have been missing. That is what I am doing today. Being the eldest, I knew this job had fallen into my hands, for it was my mother's job before it was mine, and my grandmother's job before that.

You would think that we all would have learned this big lesson years ago, because it is the same lesson that repeats itself over and over again: to spend time with family and loved ones while they are still living.

Though I am unable to attend this family gathering in person, I am attending it in spirit. It makes me smile to see everyone together in one room – and just to see me! I love my family more than anything, and hopefully this, my funeral, will bring them back together again.

In life, the irreplaceable are usually the overlooked. Though life can be busy, never forget to set aside time to spend with your loved ones. Those moments will be cozy memories to keep you company when they are no longer able to.

Well, the show's about to start, so it is time for me to bid farewell! I don't want to miss a moment of this reunion, for they happen so infrequently, but maybe today will change that!

THE SPIRIT OF GIVING

Snow softly drifted to the ground as shoppers rushed from store to store, buying up anything that was left to give to their loved ones. Cheryl looked around at all the chaos. Over the years, she had slowly lost what had made Christmas special to her. Christmas today seemed overwhelming. People bought gifts to give to each other, expecting a gift in return. They got together for Christmas dinners but left right after they finished eating. No one seemed to even send cards anymore. She walked down the sidewalk to the next shop, doing it more as routine than anything. She was doing what she did every year – she bought gifts, wrapped gifts, sent out cards, and hosted a holiday dinner at her home. Though her holidays looked and seemed perfect, the feeling wasn't there anymore. Something was missing, but what was it?

After waiting in line for 30 minutes with her items, she walked outside with her bags. She sighed with relief as this was her last stop. Cheryl made her way through the crowded sidewalk to her car. It was dark out now. The streetlamps illuminated the falling snow creating sparkling cones below them.

Cheryl grasped her car key and turned it, but nothing happened. She tried a few more times, but her car just wouldn't start. She left her car and made her way down the sidewalk toward the car repair shop. Though it was only a few blocks away, with all the people flooding the sidewalks, it was going to take her a while to get there.

As she slowly made her way down the sidewalk, Cheryl lost herself in her thoughts, thinking about the holidays. She thought about all the gifts she gave people, and how underwhelmed they seemed with them even though she worked hard to get them the perfect gifts. She frowned as she thought about the two Christmas cards she had received, even though she had sent out 44. Christmas had lost its meaning. Suddenly, her feet slid out from under her, and she came crashing down onto the icy pavement. People continued walking past her. Some looked and giggled, but for the most part, it seemed like she didn't even exist. Her hand hurt, so she sat there and took off her glove to make sure it was ok.

"Are you ok, miss?"

Cheryl turned around to see an old man wearing old torn clothing standing next to her. With a warm smile, he held his hand out to her, offering to help her up. His gloves were torn, showing his rough skin through them. She grasped his hand and he helped her stand up.

"Thank you so much," she said. "I'm ok. My car won't start, so I was just headed over there to see if they can get it running again."

"Oh, ok. That's too bad about your car – I hope they fix it for you."

"Me too," said Cheryl. She smiled at the man and turned to walk away.

"Merry Christmas, miss!" he said with cheer.

Cheryl couldn't help but smile even wider. "A very Merry Christmas to you too!" she said. She watched the old man smile and walk away toward a shopping cart full of plastic bags, blankets, and other items. Her smile faded as she watched him sit down in the snow next to the cart. People walked passed him like he wasn't even there. Every now and then, a kid would point at the man. The parents would rush their kids past.

She looked at her watch – the car place would close soon, so she rushed there to get her car the attention it needed. They towed her car to the shop. Cheryl waited in the warm waiting room, thinking about the cold old man outside. She thought about his kindness and his cheery attitude. He didn't seem to have a thing in the world, but somehow, he seemed happy. All of a sudden, she got an idea. She rushed out into the shop and grabbed the shopping bags out of her car. She went down the street and returned "gift" after "gift" to each store, and then rushed over to where the old man sat. The sidewalks had fewer people now. The snow sparkled on the ground around him as he looked up at her with a smile.

"Can I help you, miss?"

Cheryl looked down at him and held out her hand. "Can I treat you to dinner at the café?" she asked.

"Oh, you don't have to do that," he said.

"I want to," she replied.

The man's smile widened, and he grasped her hand. He stood up and dusted the snow off of his tattered jacket.

"I just need to grab something in this store," said Cheryl. The old man waited outside as she ran in. Cheryl purchased a new jacket, gloves, and other winter apparel for the man. She also purchased a few gift cards to local restaurants. Cheryl bounced out of the shop smiling and handed the items to the man.

"Here, these are for you," she said.

The man looked at her in awe. "You really didn't have to do that," he said.

Cheryl looked at the man and smiled. "You were kind enough to lend me a hand when I needed it, so I wanted to return the favor."

The old man smiled merrily and the two of them walked through the glistening wonderland together. As they walked toward the little café, she looked over at the old man and felt something she hadn't in years. The spirit of Christmas and the spirit of giving were set ablaze in her heart once again. She felt a warmth in her soul that was indescribable. This was it, she thought. This was why the old man was so happy. Though he had little to give, he gave what he could: his kindness.

THE FORGOTTEN

"Grandma! Grandma!"

Margret smiled as she watched a young girl run into the room with excitement. Her heart illuminated with joy as she watched the youthful child skip excitedly up to an old woman across the room. The old woman smiled.

Margret turned her gaze to the window and watched the snowflakes softly fall to the ground outside. It had been months since her family had visited her at the nursing home. She told other residents that she understood her family's absence, saying, "They are busy." She couldn't lie to herself though. Deep inside, she was sad. She felt like an outdated toy shoved into a box of old forgotten items. Though she knew her family hadn't completely forgotten about her, like the old box of items, she knew there were probably more exciting things for them to spend their time on than her.

Margret spent her days watching other residents receive surprise visits from their loved ones. She couldn't help but be a little envious of them. She sat in view of the door, waiting for her family to visit her. She recounted the last time her daughter visited. Like most of the visitors of the home, it too was a surprise visit. For some reason, people didn't find importance in visiting their elders, so they visited infrequently. If only they knew how much it meant to them. She knew how much it meant to her.

Though her daughter's last visit was brief, it kept her going. It gave her something to smile inside about each morning, and something cozy to reminisce about each night. But, over time, the memories of the visits would slowly become bittersweet because as much as the visits reminded her of how much she was loved, when the memories grew distant, they also reminded her how forgotten she was. Though she was around many other residents in the home, she had never felt more alone in her life.

One sunny spring morning, Margret fell faint and was rushed to the hospital. She awoke to flowers and balloons next to her bedside, but most importantly, to her daughter's hand holding hers. She felt a breath of life fill her lungs as happiness overtook her. She looked over at her daughter's face noticing smudged makeup around her eyes.

"Sweetie, what's wrong?" Margret asked, rubbing her daughter's hand in hers.

Her daughter sat in silence and just looked at her. The haunted look in her daughter's eyes said it all. Margret hated seeing the pain in her daughter's eyes, but the painful look oddly comforted her, for it showed that her daughter did truly care.

Margret nodded and looked across the room. She breathed in and breathed out slowly, accepting her fate - she was dying. Margret sat in self-pity for a moment, when suddenly she thought of something she wanted to do. She shook the sorrow from her heart and her eyes brightened.

"Honey, can you do something for me?" she asked.

"Sure Mom, whatever you want."

Margret smiled. "I know you are really busy with your books, but I have a story I want you to write."

Her daughter took intricate notes as Margret shared her heart and dreams with her. She learned a lot about her mother, and felt sorry she hadn't visited more often. Over the next two and a half weeks, her daughter visited her daily to talk and take notes on the story. Margret was so happy to finally spend time with her daughter. She was the happiest she had been in years. Though her happiness grew, her condition worsened, until one stormy summer night, she drifted off in her sleep and never woke up.

On the one-year anniversary of her mother's hospital stay, her daughter released what would be her mother's legacy: *The Invisible*, a book that shined a spotlight on how lonely life could be in a nursing home. With success beyond her wildest dreams, the book brought nursing home residents back into their families' lives once more. *The Invisible* shed light onto a forgotten topic - making an unforgettably wonderful impact on the lives of elders all around the world.

The forgotten and the invisible became the remembered, the visited, the seen, the heard, and the loved.

BOB AND GLORIA

Gloria

As it usually does, this ending began with a phone call. It was 3am. Gloria awoke, startled by the ringing of the phone. There was an understood rule –when the phone rang at this hour, the news wasn't going to be good. She reached over to her nightstand and quickly picked up the phone. She sat there silently in bed as she took in the bad news. Bob, someone she once knew well, was in his final stages of life. Her instant reaction to this news, was one of annoyance. Bob and Gloria had a past – and not a good one. She sat in the quiet of the early morning hours in anger. She had made a decision years ago that she never wanted to see him again, and now, of course, he was dying.

After an hour, her thoughts transitioned to slight sorrow. She didn't like this feeling, nor did she understand it. Why would she feel sad about someone she didn't ever want to see again? Guilt started creeping into her thoughts too. It was a complex storm of emotions, and she was angry it was happening at all. Why did Bob have to do this to her? Weren't all the harsh words and encounters

73

they had shared in the past enough? She had
planned on being angry at him for good. She never
really thought about him ever dying.

Bob

Bob lay in the hospital bed. Knowing his time on
this earth was nearing its end, he rested deep in
thought about the past. A certain clarity came to
him in that moment. In the end, only what was real
truly mattered. He thought about the people he had
hurt in the past, and for the first time in his life, he
felt sorry for his actions. He thought about Gloria,
and the tiffs they had that kept them apart all these
years. He was truly sorry and hoped for her
forgiveness. He didn't want to leave his life with
loose ends. He knew how angry she was, so he
wasn't sure she would ever give him a chance to
apologize. He didn't expect her to understand this
clarity he found in his last days – it was a certain
epiphany most never experience outside of this
situation. Never-the-less, hope rested shakily in his
heart.

Gloria

The sun rose on the horizon outside her window.
She felt better after she had a chance to rest and let
go of her problems for a while. She still was pretty

set on not visiting Bob. She was still angry about the past.

Gloria went about her day, going through the usual daily tasks. A small amount of guilt uncomfortably sat in her stomach. After a while, she got tired of this feeling and decided to visit Bob, but only to get rid of that bad feeling – she was doing this for herself. She got dressed, grabbed her purse, and left.

Bob & Gloria

She parked her car and made her way into the hospital. Her heart pounded in her chest. She was so mad that she had to do this. She found the hospital room and stood staring at it from a distance for a little while. She thought about all the things Bob had done in the past – it made her want to turn around and leave.

A nurse saw her staring at the door. "Are you family?"

"Yes," Gloria replied.

The nurse smiled, walked up to the door and opened it. "Well, come on in!"

Gloria took a deep breath and walked into the room. The moment she saw Bob, her heart sank. A feeling of sorrow and love rushed in and pushed out all her anger. The clarity that Bob had experienced had come to her as well. In these final moments, what had happened in the past didn't seem to matter anymore. She didn't see someone she was angry at lying there. She saw someone scared. She saw someone vulnerable. For the first time, she truly realized these were their final moments together, and these moments were meant for love.

Gloria looked at Bob's face, and his expression said everything. He was sorry. She breathed in and out and forced herself to keep the sadness in her heart from showing. She smiled and gently gave him a hug.

"I'm sorry," he said. "And I'm very glad you came." He smiled sincerely.

Gloria nodded her head and smiled back. She was glad she had come too.

Years later, this final encounter had transformed her feelings toward Bob, and she held onto those warm final memories of him with fondness.

TRADITIONALLY: A CHRISTMAS STORY

It was Christmas Eve night. Audrey looked out the window at the silent streets. She knew what tomorrow was, but other than her excitement for receiving gifts, she couldn't wait for Christmas Day to be over. She thought about Christmases of the past, and how year after year, her parents did the same old things. Audrey stared unenthusiastically out the window at the falling snow as she ran through the list of traditions she would have to endure, yet again. Her day would start out with the usual family breakfast of pancakes arranged to look like snowmen with raisin faces. She rolled her eyes. Then they would take their annual Christmas Day photo in their pajamas – this tradition year after year she despised more and more. Next, they would go to her grandparent's house where they would spend the day trying to ice skate on the lake and go sledding down the hill. After nearly freezing, they would come inside and have hot cocoa by the fire and play a board game – surely something that would take forever. Audrey shook her head in annoyance. Then, after the usual Christmas supper, they would pass gifts out to one another and unwrap them. The final tradition of Christmas Day was for Grandpa to place the star on top of the Christmas tree – you know, so they could enjoy looking at it for the two seconds that were left of the day. After goodbyes that felt like hours, they would finally go home.

Audrey walked over to her bed and lay down in exhaustion. She couldn't wait for Christmas to be over. The blankets where soft and cozy beneath her, and soon, she drifted off into a deep slumber.

Light illuminated the room. Audrey sat up and looked around. She glanced at a clock – it was 10:00am already. She quickly got out of bed. Her Mom was supposed to wake her at 8:30am. Something else was strange as well – this wasn't her room. She walked up to the door and opened it.

"Good morning, Audrey!" said a cheery young woman.

"Morning," she replied. Her voice sounded different. Audrey looked past the woman at the rest of the room. It was full of elderly women and men. Some sat drinking coffee, and others chatted with each other.

"Do you need help getting to the table for breakfast?" the woman asked.

Audrey looked down at her hands, and in an instant, all the strange happenings were explained. She wasn't 17 anymore. In fact, she must have been in her 80s. She started to panic.

"Oh, hey, it's alright," said the woman, noticing her panic. The woman took her by the arm gently and helped her across the room to the table. A steaming cup of coffee was set in front of her.

"Would you like any cream or sugar?"

Audrey looked up. "Yes, thank you."

The woman sat the cream and a few packets of sugar on the table.

Audrey sat quietly. At first, she was sorrowful for her lost youth. She thought of all the superficial disadvantages of being her new age. She looked at the calendar on the wall. The staff had a magnet to indicate the days, and today was Christmas Eve. She added some sugar and cream to her coffee and stirred. She watched as the light cream swirled into the darkness of the coffee, brightening it.

The day felt strange. She didn't know what to do, so most of the day she watched TV. She kept to herself as much as she could, but that evening at supper, a resident sat next to her.

"Hi there! My name's Celia."

Audrey wanted to move, or make up an excuse to be rushed, but when she looked into the hopeful eyes of Celia, she couldn't.

"Hi Celia, I'm Audrey."

"Very nice to meet you! Such a beautiful Christmas Eve it was, wasn't it?" Celia looked at her with a happy smile.

"Yes, yes it was."

Celia looked at her with a large grin. "And tomorrow is finally Christmas Day! Oh, how I love Christmas!"

Audrey smiled and took a bite of her food.

"You know," started Celia, "we had the best Christmases – the very best. My father used to take us to this tree farm to pick a tree. I remember playing with my big sister; we would play tag in the pines. Dad would of course try to get our attention focused on picking a tree, and when we started looking, it took hours! It was such a large tree farm, and I wanted the perfect one." Celia laughed with a childlike glee. "My dad would laugh because I always seemed to pick out the biggest trees, and we only had eight-foot ceilings in our house. Finally, we would all agree on a tree and take it home. When we got there, Mom would be waiting by the fireplace with bowls of popcorn and cranberries. It was a truly old-fashioned way to decorate the tree, but Mom loved the look and we liked making the garlands. We would spend most of Christmas day making decorations for the tree, and finally, we would decorate it."

Celia looked off into the distance, lost in nostalgia. "But, it has been years and years since then. Truth be told, I miss those days. I miss those traditions. Did your family have any traditions?"

Audrey looked at her and shared the traditional schedule for her Christmases. Only upon finishing did she realize something – Christmas was going to be different this year. I'm sure it will be nice doing my own thing for a change, she thought. After they finished chatting, she said goodnight to Celia and made her way back to her room to get ready for bed.

That evening, Audrey sat next to the window and looked out at the silent glistening world outside.

She thought about how tomorrow was Christmas Day, and finally she would get to do whatever she wanted this year. If she wanted some family time, she could always call her parents... She paused for a moment. For some reason it hadn't even occurred to her until just now, but her parents most likely were no longer living. A silent calm fell over her. She gently lay down on her bed. A tear slid down her cheek as she closed her eyes.

She awoke to bright sunlight again. She looked outside at the wintery landscape. Seeing the snow-covered homes in the distance reminded her of the Christmas villages her mother used to set up each year.

Audrey got dressed and walked out of her room.

"Merry Christmas!" said the cheery woman.

"Merry Christmas to you too," Audrey replied back.

Audrey walked over to the tables and sat down to breakfast. She stared down at the plate of eggs and toast as she thought about the traditional snowman pancakes of her past. It's fine, she thought. She ate breakfast, then walked over to sit in front of the TV. She watched TV for a while, but had a hard time focusing on the shows. She thought about how, right about now, she would be ice skating and sledding at her grandparent's lake home. A longing grew quietly inside her.

She decided to play cards by herself. She did this for a few hours, then went back to trying to watch TV. As the world outside grew dim, Audrey sat down to supper. She looked down at her plate and reminisced about her grandmother's Christmas dinners. She thought about how they used to pass gifts out and open them. She lost herself in a moment of her own, but suddenly realized she was the last one in the room. She looked around. Everyone must have gone to bed, she thought. In the far distant corner rested a Christmas tree. It was covered in a variety of ornaments, kind of like her grandparent's tree was. She looked at it funny - it seemed as if they had forgotten to put a topper on it. It bothered her for some reason. It was Christmas night, and that tree still had no topper. She went in her room, grabbed a scissors and paper, and sat back down at the table. She thought about her grandfather as she cut out a star. Her eyes glistened over as she walked over to the tree, remembering her past tradition of her grandfather putting the star on their tree on Christmas night. She pushed a chair up to the tree, stood on it, and with eyes full of tears, placed the paper star atop the Christmas tree. She stood there in a quiet sadness for a moment. She never realized it before, but traditions have a lifetime. For some reason, she thought they would go on forever – that they would always be there. She looked at that star and thought to herself, *we grow up with traditions, and sometimes fight them because we get bored of them and want to do something new, something better. But when traditions come to an end, they turn into a missing piece of an annual celebration, a memory. We can try to continue traditions, but in some ways, they partially become new traditions because part of what made them special and familiar were the people we shared them with. And unfortunately, people don't live forever.* She thought about her family. She took in a deep breath and wished she had appreciated those traditions more than she had.

Audrey looked a while longer at the star she made and it warmly put a smile on her face. She sniffled and wiped her tears. I should probably get to bed, she thought. She took a step and suddenly lost her balance – falling quickly to the floor.

With a gasp, she threw her arms out while sitting up in haste. Audrey grasped at her bedpost as she nearly fell out of bed. She looked out into the room – it was her old bedroom! The sunlight slowly peaked above the horizon in the distance, casting an ember glow all around her. She got up and ran into the hall to look in the mirror – she was 17 again! An overwhelming happiness blossomed inside her. The house was silent. She snuck into the China cabinet and quietly started setting the table for breakfast.

"Hi, honey. You're up early!"

"Merry Christmas, Mom!" Audrey said with a large smile. Her Mom looked uncertain with her daughter's unusual cheery attitude but decided to go with it. They embraced in a warm hug. Audrey watched as her Mom gathered the supplies to make their traditional snowman pancakes. She smiled with a new-found appreciation for these precious annual moments. With a heart full of love, she went into the kitchen to help her mom. The two of them laughed and made memories together – memories Audrey would later look back on and realize were more valuable than gold.

FRACTURE

In a little town, nestled quietly in the hillside, rested a small shop. Full of many unique decorations, the shop was visited by local residents in search of items for their homes. The shop owner chose each item he displayed in his shop, knowing that someone would love them. He sat in a chair behind the front counter, watching and listening to his customers who stopped in.

A section of four large vases were nestled between two shelves. Three vases were beige with subtle floral designs. The other vase was bright blue with vibrant painted scenery on it. Passersby would regularly comment on the beige vases as they walked by, saying how beautiful they were, and how because they were neutral colored, they fit in more. But as for the bright blue vase, it received remarks that mocked it. Customers would say things like: "Who would ever buy that?" and "That belongs in the trash." People laughed at the blue vase because of its difference from what was commonly accepted as household decoration colors.

Weeks went by and the beige vases stood tall and proud. They knew they were beautiful because people said so. The blue vase, however, took each harsh word and comment to heart, and with each comment, it cracked slightly. Each time the blue vase cracked, the beige vases would point it out, causing the blue vase to fracture a little more each time. They enjoyed the fact that the blue vase was cracking, because by contrast, it made them look even better.

A few more weeks went by. As usual, customer after customer complimented on the beauty of the beige vases and made fun of the blue vase. The blue vase seemed to begin to slouch. It tried to stand tall and proud like the other beige vases, but the harsh words it received daily were taking a toll on its heart, and it was sure that someday soon, it would break completely.

One day, the shop owner was dusting his merchandise and came across the section of vases. He smiled at the beige vases, but his smile faded when he looked at the poor blue vase. It was covered in tiny cracks that crawled across its once flawless surface. He picked up the vase carefully and took it to his workshop in the back. The blue vase let out a slow exhale, for it was sure its end was near. The man set the vase on a counter in front of a large mirror. The blue vase looked at itself.

Those tiny fractures that were once bad feelings on the inside, were now faintly visible on the outside. It stared at itself, wishing it was a different color, wishing it was like the other vases that people seemed to like more.

The man walked back up to the vase, but instead of throwing it away, he began restoring it.

"You really are a great-looking vase," he said while he worked. "I know some people can't see your unique beauty, but many people only know how to judge what they don't understand."

He continued fixing the vase, but what he didn't know is that the vase was listening to his kind words.

"I can see your beauty – that is why I chose you for my shop. There are different kinds of beauty. Some types are more misunderstood because of their uniqueness."

He picked up a brush and continued, "Now, don't tell the other vases I said this, but in my opinion, your uniqueness is what makes you stand out from all the rest. Sure, you may receive criticism from those who don't understand your one-of-a-kind qualities, but that doesn't make you any less valuable than the rest."

The man completed his restoration of the blue vase. He walked proudly with it back to the shelf and placed it next to the others once more. The blue vase felt better now – not only because it was fixed, but because of the caring words of the shop owner.

The next few days, when people walked past, the blue vase stood tall and proud like the others. The harsh words it received didn't seem to bother it anymore. The beige vases were unsure of this new-found confidence the blue vase had, and it made them a little unsure of their own beauty.

One bright summer day, a woman walked into the shop. She walked around for a while, until her eyes met the blue vase. Her smile grew as she walked up to it. "Oh my, this is just stunning!" she said with excitement. Without hesitation, she picked it up and brought it to the front counter. "I absolutely love this. It is just perfect!"

"I'm glad you like it. It is definitely one of my favorites," replied the shop owner with a smile.

The woman handled the vase with care, and when she got home, she displayed it on her entry table.

"There!" she said with enthusiasm. "Now you'll be the first thing people see when they walk in!"

The woman bounced away with happiness into another room, leaving the vase to its thoughts. The little blue vase sat there proudly and smiled inside.

RETOUCHED

I was obsessed with perfection. At first, the perfection I chased was achievable; things like better skin and a magazine-worthy home. But eventually, perfection began running faster than I could, and I fell behind. Perfection is never satisfied – it always demands more. I not only wanted perfect skin, but impossibly perfect skin. I not only wanted a magazine-worthy house, I wanted a house that would stay as perfect as those in the magazines, not just for a quick photo.

What the world never tells you is that everything "perfect" is retouched. What do I mean by this? I mean everything "perfect" in the world is just a little fake. Every magazine photo we compare ourselves to has been airbrushed beyond possibility and taken in the most perfect lighting with the best makeup. Those homes we want our homes to look like? These homes know no life – no kids, no dogs. These homes don't know how busy life is for the average person - for the real person. They really aren't homes. They are nonfunctional, "empty" lifeless spaces.

The so-called perfection of the world wants us to be just like them, but why isn't true perfection sold to us? The answer is a little disappointing. It is because shallow sells better than deep. Those who tell us what perfection is, have come to know this public secret. They know people will chase after perfect looks. They know people will chase after the perfect home. They don't want you to know that imperfect is the real perfect.

You should look at life like looking at an antique. With antiques, the imperfections are called character. This character is loved, and the showing of a life lived makes each item more unique and worth even more in their own way. People fall in love with the scars each antique has. People fall in love with the details that make them different than everything else.

There is beauty in what is real – more beauty than can be found in what is fake. Think about those in your life whom you love unconditionally. Do you love them because they have perfect skin or the perfect home? Or do you love them for more real reasons?

Knowing your answer to this, you can know why those in your life love you. It's not your perfection they love; it's your realness.

You know why nature is so beautiful? *It is imperfect.*

Made in United States
North Haven, CT
29 October 2022

26075865R00061